THE RIVER BANK
and
THE OPEN ROAD

KENNETH GRAHAME

Illustrated by Ernest H. Shepard

Aladdin Books
Macmillan Publishing Company
New York

Maxwell Macmillan International Publishing Group
New York   Oxford   Singapore   Sydney

First Aladdin Books edition 1991

The Wind in the Willows originally published 1908 by Charles Scribner's Sons
Text copyright © 1991 Methuen Children's Books
This presentation copyright © 1991 Methuen Children's Books
Line illustrations copyright © 1933 Charles Scribner's Sons, renewal
copyright © 1961 E. H. Shepard. Coloring-in copyright © 1970, 1971
by E. H. Shepard and Methuen Children's Books Ltd.

Aladdin Books
Macmillan Publishing Company
866 Third Avenue
New York, NY 10022

The River Bank and *The Open Road* first published in this format 1991
by Methuen Children's Books.

Printed in Hong Kong by Wing King Tong

1 2 3 4 5 6 7 8 9 10

Library of Congress CIP data is available

ISBN 0-689-71496-3

THE RIVER BANK

The Mole had been working very hard all the morning, spring-cleaning his little home. First with brooms, then with dusters; then on ladders with a brush and a pail of whitewash; till he had splashes of whitewash all over his black fur, an aching back and weary arms. Spring was moving in the air above and in the earth below and around him, penetrating even his dark and lowly little house with its spirit of divine discontent and longing. It was small wonder, then, that he suddenly flung down his brush on the floor, said "Bother!" and "Hang spring-cleaning!" and bolted out of the house.

He scraped and scratched and scrabbled and scrooged, working busily with his little paws and muttering, "Up we go! Up we go!" till at last, pop! his snout came out into the sunlight, and he found himself rolling in the warm grass of a great meadow. "This is fine!" he said to himself. "This is better than whitewashing!" and he jumped off all his four legs at once, in the joy of living and the delight of spring without its cleaning.

He thought his happiness was complete when, as he meandered aimlessly along, suddenly he stood by the edge of a full-fed river. Never in his life had he seen a river before. All was a-shake and a-shiver—glints and gleams and sparkles, rustle and swirl, chatter and bubble. The Mole was bewitched. As he sat on the grass, a dark hole in the bank opposite, just above the water's edge, caught his eye. Then, as he looked, a small face appeared. A little brown face, with whiskers.

It was the Water Rat!

"Hullo, Mole!" he said. "Would you like to come over?"

"Oh, it's all very well to *talk*," said the Mole, rather peevishly, he being new to riverside life and its ways.

The Rat said nothing, but stepped into a little boat which the Mole had not observed and sculled smartly across. "Now then, step lively!" he said, holding up his fore-paw as the Mole stepped gingerly down, and the Mole, to his surprise and rapture, found himself seated in the stern of a real boat.

"Do you know," he said, "I've never been in a boat before in all my life."

"What?" cried the Rat, open-mouthed. "Never been in a—you never—well, I—what have you been doing then?"

"Is it so nice as all that?" asked the Mole shyly.

"Nice? It's the *only* thing," said the Water Rat solemnly. "Believe me, my friend, there is *nothing* half so much worth doing as messing about in boats. Look here! Supposing we drop down the river together, and have a long day of it?"

The Mole waggled his toes from sheer happiness. "*What* a day I'm having!" he said. "Let us start at once!"

"Hold hard a minute, then!" said the Rat and climbed up into his hole above. He reappeared with a fat, wicker luncheon-basket.

"What's inside it?" asked the Mole, wriggling with curiosity.

"There's cold chicken inside it," replied the Rat briefly; "coldtonguecoldham-coldbeefpickledgherkinssaladfrenchrolls-cresssandwidgespottedmeatgingerbeer-lemonadesodawater—"

"O stop, stop," cried the Mole in ecstasies. "This is too much!"

"Do you really think so?" inquired the Rat. "It's only what I always take on these little excursions."

"All this is so new to me," said the Mole. "Do you really live by the river? What a jolly life!"

"By it and with it and on it and in it," said the Rat. "It's brother and sister to me, and company, and food and drink. Lord! the times we've had together!

"Now then! Here's our backwater, where we're going to lunch."

It was so very beautiful that the Mole could only hold up both fore-paws and gasp, "O my! O my! O my!"

The Rat helped the Mole safely ashore, and swung out the luncheon-basket. The Mole begged to be allowed to unpack it all by himself; and the Rat was very pleased to indulge him, and to sprawl at full length on the grass and rest.

When all was ready, the Rat said, "Now pitch in, old fellow!" and the Mole was very glad to, for he had started his spring-cleaning at a very early hour that morning, as people *will* do, and had not paused for bite or sup.

"What are you looking at?" said the Rat presently, when the edge of their hunger was somewhat dulled.

"I am looking," said the Mole, "at a streak of bubbles that I see travelling along the surface of the water."

"Bubbles? Oho!" said the Rat in an inviting sort of way.

A broad glistening muzzle showed itself above the edge of the bank, and the Otter hauled himself out and shook the water from his coat.

"Greedy beggars!" he observed, making for the provisions. "Why didn't you invite me, Ratty?"

"This was an impromptu affair," explained the Rat. "By the way—my friend Mr Mole."

"Proud, I'm sure," said the Otter, and the two animals were friends forthwith.

"Such a rumpus everywhere!"

continued the Otter. "All the world
seems out on the river today. Toad's out
in his brand-new boat; new togs, new
everything!"

The two animals looked at each other
and laughed.

"Once, it was nothing but sailing," said the Rat. "Then he tired of that and took to punting. Last year it was house-boating. We all had to go and stay with him in his house-boat, and pretend we liked it. It's all the same, whatever he takes up; he gets tired of it, and starts on something fresh."

"Such a good fellow, too," remarked the Otter: "But no stability—especially in a boat!"

From where they sat they could get a glimpse of the main stream; and just then a boat flashed into view, the rower—a short, stout figure—splashing badly and

rolling a good deal, but working his hardest. The Rat stood up and hailed him, but Toad—for it was he—shook his head and settled sternly to his work.

"He'll be out of the boat in a minute if he rolls like that," said the Rat, sitting down again.

"Of course he will," chuckled the Otter.

Just then, an errant May-fly swerved past. There was a swirl of water and a *cloop!* and the May-fly disappeared. So did the Otter.

"Well, well," said the Rat, "I suppose we ought to be moving. I wonder which of us had better pack the luncheon-basket?"

He did not speak as if he was frightfully eager for the treat.

"O, please let me," said the Mole. So, of course, the Rat let him. The afternoon sun was getting low as the Rat sculled gently homewards in a dreamy mood.

The Mole was full of lunch and already quite at home in a boat (so he thought). Presently he said, "Ratty! Please, *I* want to row, now!"

The Rat shook his head with a smile. "Not yet," he said—"wait till you've had a few lessons. It's not so easy as it looks."

The Mole was quiet for a minute or two. But he began to feel more and more jealous of Rat. He jumped up and seized the sculls, so suddenly, that the Rat was taken by surprise and fell backwards off his seat with his legs in the air.

The triumphant Mole took his place, flung his sculls back with a flourish, and made a great dig at the water. He missed the surface altogether, his legs flew up above his head and—*sploosh!* Over went the boat.

O my, how cold the water was, and O, how *very* wet it felt. Then a firm paw gripped him by the back of his neck. It was the Rat, and he was laughing.

He propelled the helpless Mole to shore and set him down on the bank, a squashy, pulpy lump of misery.

The dismal Mole, wet without and ashamed within, trotted about till he was fairly dry, while the Rat recovered the boat and dived for the luncheon-basket.

As they set off again, the Mole said in a low voice, "Ratty, my friend! I am very sorry indeed for my foolish conduct. My heart quite fails me when I think how I might have lost that beautiful luncheon-basket. Will you forgive me?"

"That's all right, bless you!" responded the Rat cheerily. "What's a little wet to a Water Rat? Don't you think any more about it; and look here! I really think you had better come and stop with me for a little time. I'll teach you to row and to swim, and you'll soon be as handy on the water as any of us."

The Mole was so touched that he could
find no voice to answer; and he had to
brush away a tear or two with the back of
his paw.

When they got home, the Rat made a
bright fire in the parlor and planted the
Mole in an arm-chair in front of it. Then
he fetched down a dressing-gown and
slippers for him and told him river stories
till supper-time.

Supper was a most cheerful meal. But shortly afterwards a terribly sleepy Mole had to be escorted upstairs by his considerate host, to the best bedroom, where he soon laid his head on his pillow in great peace and contentment.

This day was only the first of many similar ones for the Mole, each of them longer and fuller of interest as the ripening summer moved onward. He learned to swim and to row, and entered into the joy of running water.

THE OPEN ROAD

One bright summer morning, the Rat was sitting on the river bank, singing a little song.

"Ratty," said the Mole suddenly, "if you please, I want to ask you a favor. Won't you take me to call on Mr Toad? I've heard so much about him, and I do so want to make his acquaintance."

"Why, certainly," said the good-natured Rat. "Get the boat out, and we'll paddle up there at once."

"It's never the wrong time to call on Toad. Early or late he's always glad to see you."

"He must be a very nice animal," observed the Mole.

"He is indeed the best of animals," replied Rat. "So good-natured and affectionate. Perhaps he's not very clever—we can't all be geniuses; and it may be that he is both boastful and conceited. But he has got some great qualities, has Toady."

Rounding a bend in the river, they
came in sight of a handsome, dignified old
house, with well-kept lawns reaching
down to the water's edge.

"There's Toad Hall," said the Rat. "Toad
is rather rich, you know, and this is really
one of the nicest houses in these parts,
though we never admit as much to Toad."

They disembarked, and strolled across the flower-decked lawns in search of Toad, whom they found resting in a wicker garden-chair with a preoccupied expression of face, and a large map spread out on his knees.

"Hooray!" he cried, jumping up on seeing them, "this is splendid!" He shook the paws of both of them warmly, never waiting for an introduction to the Mole. "You don't know how lucky it is, your turning up just now!"

"Let's sit quiet a bit, Toady!" said the Rat, throwing himself into an easy chair, while the Mole took another by the side of him and made some civil remark about Toad's "delightful residence".

"Finest house on the whole river," cried Toad boisterously. "Or anywhere else, for that matter," he could not help adding.

Here the Rat nudged the Mole. The Toad saw him do it, and turned very red. Then Toad burst out laughing.

"All right, Ratty," he said. "It's only my way, you know. Now look here. You've got to help me. It's most important!"

"It's about your rowing, I suppose," said the Rat, with an innocent air. "You're getting on fairly well, though you splash a good bit still."

"O, pooh! boating!" interrupted the Toad, in great disgust. "I've given that up *long* ago. No, I've discovered the real thing, the only genuine occupation for a lifetime. I propose to devote the remainder of mine to it. Come with me, dear Ratty, and your friend also, and you shall see what you shall see!"

He led the way to the stable-yard and there, drawn out of the coach-house, they saw a gypsy caravan, shining with newness, painted a canary-yellow picked out with green, and red wheels.

"There you are!" cried the Toad, straddling and expanding himself. "There's real life for you. The open road, the dusty highway. Here today, up and off to somewhere else tomorrow! Travel, change, interest, excitement! The whole world before you. And mind, this is the finest cart of its sort that was ever built. Come inside and look at the details. Planned 'em all myself, I did!"

It was indeed very compact and comfortable. The Mole was tremendously excited, and followed him eagerly up the steps. The Rat only snorted.

"All complete!" said the Toad

triumphantly. "You see—everything you can possibly want—letter-paper, bacon, jam, cards and dominoes. You'll find," he continued, as they descended the steps again, "that nothing whatever has been forgotten, when we make our start this afternoon."

"I beg your pardon," said the Rat slowly, "but did I overhear you say something about '*we,*' and '*start,*' and '*this afternoon*'?"

"Now, dear good old Ratty," said the Toad imploringly, "you know you've *got* to come. I can't possibly manage without you. I want to show you the world!"

"I don't care," said the Rat doggedly. "I'm not coming, and that's flat. And Mole's going to do as I do, aren't you, Mole?"

"Of course I am," said the Mole loyally. "All the same, it sounds as if it might have been rather fun," he added wistfully. Poor Mole! He had fallen in love with the canary-colored cart and all its little fittings.

The Rat wavered.

"Come and have some lunch," said Toad, "and we'll talk it over."

During luncheon the Toad painted the prospects of the trip and the joys of the open life and the roadside in such glowing colors that the Mole could hardly sit in his chair for excitement. Somehow, it soon seemed taken for granted by all three of them that the trip was a settled thing; and the Rat allowed his good-nature to override his personal objections. He could not bear to disappoint his two friends.

When they were quite ready, the now triumphant Toad led his companions to the paddock and set them to capture the old gray horse, who had been told off by Toad for the dustiest job in this

dusty expedition. He frankly preferred the paddock, and took a deal of catching.

At last the horse was caught and harnessed, and they set off, all talking at once.

It was a golden afternoon.

Good-natured wayfarers stopped to say nice things about their beautiful cart; and rabbits held up their fore-paws, and said, "O my! O my! O my!"

Late in the evening, tired and happy and miles from home, they drew up on a remote common, and ate their simple supper sitting on the grass by the side of the cart.

After so much open air and excitement the Toad slept very soundly, and no amount of shaking could rouse him out of bed next morning. So the Mole and Rat turned to and the hard work had all been done by the time Toad appeared on the scene, remarking what a pleasant easy life it was they were all leading now.

Their way lay across country by
narrow lanes, and it was not till the
afternoon that they came out on the high
road. There disaster sprang out on them.

They were strolling along the high road
when far behind them they heard a faint
warning hum, like the drone of a distant
bee. Glancing back, they saw a small
cloud of dust advancing on them at
incredible speed, while from out of the
dust a faint *Poop-poop!* wailed.

In an instant the peaceful scene was changed, and with a blast of wind and a whirl of sound that made them jump for the nearest ditch, it was on them! The *poop-poop* rang in their ears and the magnificent motor-car possessed all earth and air for the fraction of a second, flung an enveloping cloud of dust that blinded and enwrapped them utterly, and then dwindled to a speck in the far distance.

The old gray horse, dreaming, as he plodded along, of his quiet paddock, reared and plunged and drove the cart backwards towards the deep ditch at the side of the road. There was a heartrending crash—and the canary-colored cart, their pride and their joy, lay on its side in the ditch, an irredeemable wreck.

The Rat danced up and down in the road. "You villains!" he shouted, shaking both fists. "You road-hogs!—I'll have the law on you!"

Toad sat down in the middle of the dusty road, his legs stretched out before him, and stared in the direction of the disappearing motor-car. His face wore a placid, satisfied expression, and at intervals he faintly murmured "Poop-poop!"

The Mole went to look at the cart, on its side in the ditch. It was indeed a sorry sight. The Rat came to help him, but their united efforts were not sufficient to right the cart. "Hey! Toad!" they cried. "Come and lend a hand, can't you!"

The Toad never answered a word, or budged from his seat in the road.

"Glorious, stirring sight!" he murmured. "The *real* way to travel! O bliss! O poop-poop! O my! O my!

"And to think I never *knew*! But *now*—
what dust-clouds shall spring up behind
me as I speed on my reckless way!"

"What are we to do with him?" asked
the Mole.

"Nothing at all," replied the Rat firmly.
"He has got a new craze, and it always
takes him that way, in its first stage. Come
on!" he said grimly. "It's five or six miles
to the nearest town, and we shall just have
to walk it.

"Now, look here, Toad! You'll have to go straight to the police-station and lodge a complaint. And then arrange for the cart to be mended."

"Police-station! Complaint!" murmured Toad dreamily. "Me *complain* of that beautiful, that heavenly vision! *Mend* the *cart!* I've done with carts forever. I never want to see the cart, or to hear of it, again."

The Rat turned from him in despair. "He's quite hopeless," he said to the Mole.

On reaching the town they went straight to the railway-station. Eventually, a slow train landed them at a station not far from Toad Hall. They escorted the spell-bound, sleep-walking Toad to his door and put him to bed. Then they got out their boat and sculled down the river home.

The following evening the Mole was sitting on the bank fishing when the Rat came strolling along to find him. "Heard the news?" he said. "There's nothing else being talked about, all along the river bank. Toad went up to Town by an early train this morning. And he has ordered a large and very expensive motor-car!"